J   Hyatt, Patricia
    Rusch.

    Coast to coast with
    Alice.

$19.95

DATE			
MAR 15 1996			
MAY 14 1996			

BAKER & TAYLOR BOOKS

Minna and Alice

Coast to Coast with Alice

by Patricia Rusch Hyatt

Carolrhoda Books, Inc. / Minneapolis

For my mother, Winnifred Rusch Hagood,
a road-runner herself

Carolrhoda Books, Inc. c/o The Lerner Group
241 First Avenue North, Minneapolis, Minnesota 55401

Library of Congress Cataloging-in-Publication Data

Hyatt, Patricia Rusch.
  Coast to coast with Alice / by Patricia Rusch Hyatt.
    p.   cm.
  Summary: Sixteen-year-old Hermine Jahns relates her experiences
traveling on the first cross-country automobile trip with a woman
driver in 1909.
  ISBN 0-87614-789-9
  1. Jahns, Hermine, 1893-   —Juvenile fiction.   2. Ramsey, Alice—
Juvenile fiction.   [Jahns, Hermine, 1893-   —Fiction.   2. Ramsey,
Alice—Fiction.   3. Automobile travel—Fiction.   4. Sex role—
Fiction.   5. Diaries.]   I. Title.
PZ7.H96754Co   1995
[Fic]—dc20   94-25750
                                                           CIP
                                                            AC

Manufactured in the United States of America
1 2 3 4 5 6 – I/JR – 00 99 98 97 96 95

A NOTE TO THE READER

Hermine Jahns was a real girl who rode across the country with Alice Ramsey in 1909. To create her journal, I drew on long-ago newspaper stories, interviews, books about slang and fads of the early 1900s, and most importantly the memoirs Alice herself wrote in 1961—more than 50 years after her historic trip. The result is this story, which is as true as I could make it. The conversations are imagined, but every event actually happened.

A number of people helped me with facts and advice: Doris and Wayne Armstrong, Marion Arenas, Bobbie Moore, Carole and Neil Prendergast, Mary Riskind, Judy Stamper, William Wong, and especially Jim Hyatt.

Alice at the wheel

June 8, 1909
Hurry Up, Tomorrow   Hackensack, New Jersey

I can't sleep. How could anybody sleep? How much
longer 'til morning? I am one of the luckiest girls alive
in the United States, the Hemisphere, the World, the
Universe, the I-don't-know. My neighborhood friend
Alice Ramsey has invited me—yes ME, Hermine Jahns
(people call me Minna)—to ride up front with her
starting tomorrow morning as she drives a motorcar
from New York City all the way to San Francisco,
California, on the Pacific Ocean! No woman driver has
tried the whole distance yet—Alice is bound to be the
first. And I'll be there too.

   Only two men have ever driven this distance before.
It took each of those fellows more than 60 days. The
roads are all wagon ruts west of the Mississippi River,
they say, and burro trails through the mountains. Great
golliwogs, won't that be an adventure? Will we find
buffalo, Indians, and cowboys? Oh, I wish tomorrow
would come sooner.

I will be the youngest of the four of us making this trip—I am going on 16—but Alice knows how much I like machines and motoring, and she's already taught me oiling and tire changing. So I will be dependable in the wilderness, like a good first mate on a ship. Unless we . . . oh, dear, there's no sense imagining bad things that could happen. Otherwise, we'd never try.

My family finally agreed to let me ride along after Alice promised we'd have chaperones. So now Alice's two sisters-in-law are coming too. They are Mrs. Nettie Powell and Mrs. Maggie Atwood, and they are maybe 30 or 40—much older than Alice or I. They are supposed to "look after us." You'd think this was going to be some sort of tea dance! The truth is, Alice doesn't need any looking after, and neither do I.

That's exactly what I told my cousin Kermit, the smarty pants, when he laughed at the whole idea of four females making this trip. He thinks we'll give up and head home on a train before we even reach the Mississippi River. "And if you should get so far," he says, "I'll eat my hat!" I hope he likes the taste of straw. Kermit doesn't know Alice and how stubborn she can be. (I mean stubborn in a good way.)

In my secret dreams, I would like to be just like Alice, and maybe I will be in a few years. She is 21 now, but she isn't prissy or bossy at all. I would say she is plucky.

Alice's family lives on our street here in Hackensack. Her father always says Alice was "born mechanical." He taught her about tools in his workshop, and then she took manual training in school instead of homemaking. She learned how to make wooden tables and hatstands rather than how to cook and sew. People think it strange for a girl to take manual training, but I think it is wonderful. I wish I'd thought of it first.

About half a year ago when Alice first learned to drive—after only two lessons!—she started taking me with her on short trips in her family's red Maxwell. Picnics mostly, or sometimes we'd go to a "run," where other drivers in Maxwells or Packards, usually, or Franklins or Cadillacs would show off how well they could back up, handle the wheel on corners, and drive around barrels and hay bales. Alice always scores very high at these meets, and we celebrate afterward with ice cream cones and iced tea—when the weather is warm, that is.

The biggest contest Alice has entered (so far) was the 150-mile Montauk Point Run on Long Island in New York. That day the road to the meet was full of some of the most curious contraptions. I saw a Piano Box Runabout, an electric car that looks like a piano on wheels; a Thomas, which resembles two bicycles locked together; and a new Buick, manufactured by some plumber who also invented the white porcelain bathtub. There were a number of Oldsmobiles whose drivers joked and sang that jolly tune "Come Away With Me, Lucille, in My Merry Oldsmobile." Instead of a steering wheel like the Maxwell, the Olds has a tiller like a sailboat.

There at Montauk, as we fully expected, Alice made

Instead of turning a steering wheel, the driver steered this 1903 Oldsmobile with a long stick, or tiller.

another perfect score. A salesman from the Maxwell car company, a Mr. Cadwallader Washburn Kelsey (whew!), watched all her turns and reverses. He came up afterward and declared she was the greatest natural woman driver he'd ever seen and that she had given him a unique idea. How would she like to be the first woman to drive across the United States?

So that's how our adventure started, and tomorrow I'll be sharing the front seat with Alice on the first-time all-women's journey across this great country, courtesy of the Maxwell-Briscoe Company. Our official starting point is the Maxwell salesroom at 1930 Broadway, in New York City, about 15 miles from home. We will be driving over rivers and mountains, wildernesses and deserts. I already feel like a pioneer—a modern twentieth-century one. Though I guess it will scare me a bit to be so far from home.

I am going to try to sleep a little now. Good night.

June 9, 1909
We're Off   *Poughkeepsie, New York*

This morning in New York City, it rained so hard there were waves blowing down Broadway. The four of us looked like fishermen in our long rubber ponchos and rubber helmets with flaps that covered our necks. The Elks' Lodge, a men's club, gave us four bunches of dripping wet pink carnations. Then we were told to line up for picture taking.

Right off the bat, the New York newspaper reporters asked us where our GUNS were. We said we weren't carrying any, thank you.

11

Then somebody wanted to know whether we had any pillows. I guess they thought we'd need dainty cushions for bouncing on the rugged, rocky trails. Alice told them if one of us wants a pillow, she'll have to board a train.

Before long, we four got tired of standing around in the rain puddles answering endless questions. All I could think was, let's go, let's go, let's go, and I guess I drummed my fingers loudly on the car door. Alice

Here we are, clutching our flowers and waiting for Alice to climb behind the wheel so we can start our adventure.

looked over at me and raised her eyebrows. Then she winked and shouted, "ALL ABOARD!"

Alice sloshed to the front of the car and gave the crank a strong whirl. There was a loud roar, and she hurried around to climb up to the front seat and push on the throttle so the engine would hum. "I was brought up not to race an engine," Alice shouted to the reporters. Then she let in the clutch stick. The wheels began to turn, and we were off! The four of us waved good-bye with our droopy flowers. (Later, when we were out of sight, we tossed them to a farm boy sitting by the road. My, was he surprised to have pink posies land in his lap!)

The rain followed us up Broadway, pounding hard on our rubbery pantasote roof. To me, the sound was like applause.

Our Maxwell touring car is a shiny beauty, and Alice has it perfectly fixed up for the trip. Most Maxwells are painted Speedster Red. But this one is a DR model, so it is painted bright green. DR stands for doctor. It must cost much more than the standard red auto, which I know is $550, because the DR is a more powerful machine, built to drive over hilly country and sandy roads that a doctor must travel to reach sick people. Alice says the steering is a bit stiff, but that's good for starting out.

The Maxwell people have exchanged the regular 14-gallon gas tank for one that holds 20 gallons. We have a rack for two extra tires on the right side of the car. And, of course, we have a tire repair kit. There's also a picnic hamper full of food like cornflakes and canned tomatoes, and a box camera. Last week Alice showed all three of us how to take pictures.

Before we began to pack, Alice told us, "This trip is not going to be a style show." So we are bringing only one small suitcase apiece. For sunny days I, like all the rest, will be wearing a two-piece fitted suit of stiff tan cloth, a large, full cap with a visor, and a silk crepe veil to tie in a bow under my chin. By the time I packed just one change of clothes plus a pretty blue blouse to dress up my suit for city wear and an extra change of underclothes and shoes, the case was full. I peeked before Nettie and Maggie latched their straps, and I saw their cut-glass jars with silver tops for face creams and toilet water. I don't have anything so fancy, only plain soap and a tortoiseshell comb and brush.

The Maxwell's gas tank is just under my seat, and one of my jobs is to keep track of our fuel level with a ruled stick. Someone should invent a device that tells you when the tank is getting empty. Nettie's been asking me to measure almost every hour. I feel like talking back, but I don't want to spoil everything the first day out. Alice whispered to me that Nettie gets nervous, and in a while I'll be able to prove to her that the fuel level goes down slowly and doesn't vanish in a poof like a magician's rabbit.

14

On the auto's left running board is a carbide generator to make the gas fumes that power our headlamps.
Yes, we are going to be able to drive after sunset! That's
something Lewis and Clark couldn't do when they
explored the West about a hundred years ago. To turn
on our headlamps, I drop special carbide pellets into the
generator; then Alice and I jump down, and I open the
front glass over the two headlamps. Alice strikes the
match and holds it to each gas escape tube until the
flame is steady. Then I snap the glass partway shut, and
we're ready to go. We will have to drive somewhat
slower at night, but our top speed in the daytime should
hit 40 miles an hour!

Leaving New York City, with the mud chains on our
tires clacking up Broadway, we headed north through
Yonkers, Dobbs Ferry, Tarrytown—where we stopped for
hot chocolate—and up the Albany Post Road toward
the state capital at Albany. The roads so far are either
dirt or crushed stone called macadam. The local photographers are hilarious to watch. They try to keep
their balance behind their tripods, while standing up in
the rear of an automobile that's sliding around on the
mud-slick road ahead of us. My mouth must be wide
open and laughing in all of today's photos.

I am writing this at Nelson House, in a dormitory
room at Vassar College in Poughkeepsie, New York,
with our first day's driving behind us. I will try to write
as often as I can, but it may have to be late at night,
after we've stopped for the day. It is impossible to hold
the pencil still when the Maxwell's moving.

June 10, 1909
Mr. Kelsey's Scheme   Amsterdam, New York

In Albany today we met the very jolly Mr. John D.
Murphy ("J. D."), a round-faced, curly-haired editor for
the *Boston Herald*. He says he has been hired by Mr.
Kelsey of the Maxwell Company to follow by train and
find us a place to stay each night. He will also send
ahead to each town the news that we are on our way.
Now how is this to work? we all wondered. I asked
Mr. Murphy if we are to be treated like the Barnum and
Bailey Circus.

Mr. Murphy shrugged and said that Mr. Kelsey is
always dreaming up ideas to sell cars, and that our trip
is one of his grandest "brainstorms." From what Mr.
Murphy told us, it's no wonder that Mr. Kelsey is the
darling of the newspapers in Philadelphia, where he
lives.

Last year he hired a cameraman to shoot moving pictures of a Maxwell driving up the 88 steps to the front
door of the Philadelphia Museum of Art. No one from
the museum gave him permission. The only reason he
got away with the stunt was that he'd hired two other
drivers to honk and shout at each other in a nearby
park, so the police would leave the museum
steps unguarded.

After that stair-step film was shown in nickelodeon
theaters all over the city, Maxwell cars sold faster than
lemonade on a midsummer day.

Then, to keep up people's interest, Mr. Kelsey made

another nickelodeon film to show how well the Maxwell brakes work. This time he told the camera-man to point his lens at a nursemaid as she crossed the street with a baby carriage. Mr. Kelsey announced he aimed to drive up really fast in a red Maxwell and stop just in the nick of time.

Who on earth would dare to pose for such a dangerous scene? It also sounded pretty foolhardy to the man with the camera. He wanted Mr. Kelsey to park the car one foot away from the nurse and the baby, then drive the car backward down the street. The finished film could be shown in reverse. That way, the nurse and baby would never be in danger.

But Mr. Kelsey said NO FAKERY for him. Then he shouted to start up the filming. The next thing the cameraman knew,

Mr. Kelsey was driving straight toward the nurse and the buggy. A few seconds later, the nurse (luckily an acrobat), the buggy, and the baby (luckily a doll) were flying through the air.

Mr. Kelsey gave in and agreed to shoot the film the cameraman's way. "And that's the only time I ever heard of Kelsey backing off from one of his tomfool ideas," J. D. told us.

Alice asked Mr. Murphy if he thought OUR trip was tomfoolery too. "No, ma'am," he said. He thought we had the grit to make it cross country. Then he bowed and stammered something about finding the telegraph office. After he left, we took off again.

The rain keeps coming down. Even driving with tire chains, we slip and slide, once just missing the side supports of a small bridge over a fast-roaring creek. I held on to my door handle for dear life, thankful that our chains did not fail us.

Our tires are about 4 inches wide and made of smooth, slick canvas. They are 56 inches apart, which matches the wagon ruts in the North, but ruts in the South and some other parts of the country can be wider, Alice says. If we find ourselves on a 60-inch country road, we'll have to ride with one wheel down in the rut and the other up on higher ground.

In places the macadam is broken in chunks, and we have to weave in and out to protect the wheels from blowouts. You should hear Nettie and Maggie screaming, "Watch out!" You'd think we were surrounded by bears.

June 11, 1909
Rain, Rain, Go Away   Auburn, New York

At last! The sky broke clear at Little Falls, New York, and we could take off those rattling chains and roll up the window protectors. We bought ourselves a sit-down lunch instead of picnicking in the car. Alice says the best restaurants are where the trolley men eat—her father told her so. We stopped at one yesterday, and thinking about that bowl of homemade vegetable soup still makes me smack my lips. Nettie stuffed her pocketbook with homemade bread, for hunger pangs in the desert, she said.

"We're a long way from the desert," Maggie told her. "That bread will turn hard as rocks."

"Then I'll feed the prairie dogs," Nettie answered, and snapped her reticule shut. Alice just winked at me.

Not only are Maxwell people meeting us along the way, but townspeople often show up to wave and cheer. Though some do come to jeer and scoff. Lately there's this fierce argument going on among the three kinds of automobile owners: the steamer drivers against the electric drivers against the gasoline-powered drivers. Oh, the electric cars are plenty quiet and smooth, but the drawback is you have to stop and recharge the batteries after every 25 miles. And although the Stanley steamers smell better on the street than the Maxwells do, they have no gears for different speeds, and it takes 15 minutes to boil the water and collect enough steam

This is a 1907 Stanley steamer, which runs on a boiler, like a tea kettle. I'd rather ride a horse—or drive a Maxwell.

to start the wheels moving. Why, your horse could get to town and back in that much time.

My Uncle Frank drives a steamer, so of course his son, my cousin Kermit, always makes fun of gasoline-driven cars. "That Maxwell company will go broke," he says. "You won't find many people who'll pay to ride sitting on top of an explosion."

What in the world? The Auburn prison warden has sent word to our hotel he wants to see us. He is on his way over.

June 13, 1909
The Strangest Invitation   Buffalo, New York

The prison warden invited us to inspect the jail after breakfast. Imagine! Nettie and Maggie said yes just to be polite, but I was very excited about seeing real bad men in the morning and had a hard time getting to sleep. We went over there early yesterday.

Inside the gates we saw a sad-faced gang of men hammering large rocks into smaller pieces. A guard kept watch over them all. There was simply no way to guess which men were once famous bandits. Alice remarked it was better to be working outside in the fresh air than stuck in those tiny cells with tiny windows. Well, there's no doubt about that. We were all happy to wave good-bye and drive away free.

We had dry roads to Buffalo. At dusk I turned on the headlamps. Maggie kept seeing "spooks" on the road, but as we drew nearer, the spooks turned out to be milk cans set out to be picked up by the creamery. Nettie said, "I told you so." She can be so preachy.

How I wish we had a better road map. There are city maps, but no one seems to have drawn one to help motorists get from town to town. Because there are few signposts, we have to rely on a handbook called the Blue Book to figure out where to turn or which fork to follow. It has no drawings or pictures. All the directions are written out. Today, trying to get to Cleveland, Ohio, we checked our Blue Book and read, "At 11.6 miles, yellow house and barn rt. Turn left." We looked and looked for that yellow house, driving back and forth for the longest time. We wondered if Alice had misread the odometer. Nettie spied a woman down the road, and we motored over to her. I asked her which road went to Cleveland. She pointed behind us. Alice told her we saw no yellow house in that direction, only a green one. The woman laughed and said the house owner decided to repaint his house last year because he was "agin' the automobile," and he planned to have some fun confusing motorists. The woman thought the man would be all right when he got an automobile himself!

That's when we learned not to trust any directions that mentioned colors. Alice said that Blue Books don't include anything west of the Missouri River, so once we cross over, our book will be useless and we will have to follow our noses.

Four proud motorists. Alice is driving, of course, and Maggie is sitting next to her. In back, Nettie is on the left and I, Minna, am on the right.

It was a surprise to see the streets of Cleveland paved with bricks. How pretty! But it must be costly to pay the bricklayers for such an immense job.

We had the shock springs checked at the Gabriel Company there. They traded our rubber-bulb honker for a new horn with four keys that plays four buglelike notes. The tune is "My Dog Has Fleas." We all tested it. (I took more turns than anyone.) Now we will really make a stir whenever we drive into a new town. Nettie is afraid we won't be dignified. Oh, bother.

A Cleveland car was going to show us the way to Illinois, but the driver had a tire blowout after lunch. He told us to go on ahead to Toledo, Ohio, without him. We did.

A few miles later, out of nowhere, this reckless Cadillac pulled around to pass us on the right, then struck and dented our hubcap. His hubcap snapped off and clattered down the road—serves him right—but he never even stopped! Our first and only (I hope) hit-and-run-away driver. We weren't frightened until we inspected the damage. Just a dent, but that one selfish driver could have ruined this whole trip. I kicked around in the grass and found his hubcap to keep for a souvenir. It's stowed under my feet.

The roads are getting awful rough. My tailbone is sore from all this bouncing. I made a pillow out of my extra skirt. Nettie said my folks wouldn't approve of the wrinkles. "But they're not here to watch," I told her.

"Better wrinkles than bruises," said Maggie. I was surprised she spoke up for me.

Across northern Indiana the flat landscape changed to hillocks of many different heights and sand dunes, I suppose from sand blown off the shores of the Great Lakes. We've seen and crossed more train tracks today than ever before. This clue tells me we're getting near CHICAGO!

June 18, 1909
Chicago!   Chicago, Illinois

So many of the shops on Michigan Avenue look brand-new compared to back home in Hackensack. The reason why, I guess, is that much of Chicago burned to the ground about 40 years ago. That's when Mrs. O'Leary's cow kicked over a lantern in a barn and started the Great Fire.

The main street of Chicago is paved with black asphalt, like in New York City. Most of the side streets are limestone slabs, which give off a white dust that chokes us as we motor along. When we began honking our fancy new horn, Nettie sat stiff as a poker and pretended she didn't know us, her nose in the air as if to say, "I only dropped from the sky into this backseat purely by accident."

This morning Alice got us up at 3 A.M. to drive 47 miles to watch what they call the Cobe Cup stock

*Nettie, next to me in back, seems to be hiding from the camera.
I wonder if she's still miffed about the horn!*

car races at Crown Point. Alice told me these are probably the first stock car races in the United States. It
was a day filled with lots of noise, squealing brakes, and
dust clouds in the hot sun. Someone gave us paper cones
filled with cracked ice made from lemonade. It was the
perfect treat. The winner of the day was Louis Chevro-
let, driving a Buick. I tried to get his autograph on my
score sheet, but the crowd around him was too thick.

At the end of the day, our freshly cleaned clothes were covered with dust and we looked like dirty raccoons with white masks when we took our goggles off. How glorious to feel spotless again after a bath in the hotel. Tomorrow we will sleep late, then shake out our dusty clothes and tour the city parks. It's now ten days gone from home. We are one-third across the great United States of America.

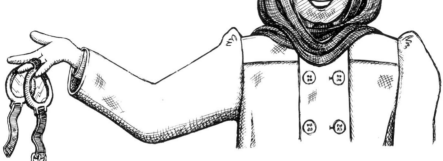

June 23, 1909
Fixing a Flat   *Rochelle, Illinois*

To cross Illinois, we've been joined by J. D. Murphy again and three motorcars full of photographers and car salesmen. Everybody wants to be a part of our trip. The driving has been pretty tame so far, except for the rain, but the locals keep telling us the roads get worse as we move farther west.

Alice and I went shopping this morning for strong towing rope, a block and tackle (to hook and lift the car

Maggie stands by ready to help while Alice changes a flat.

out of ditches if we need to), and short shovels. Then the four of us climbed aboard and led the parade of news people west over farm roads that crossed cornfields divided by small creeks. I counted 12 scarecrows, and then the Maxwell started to wobble. It was a flat tire!

Maggie asked Alice if she wanted to use the tank of compressed air. But Alice said no because we may need to save that air for flat tires in the desert or in the rain. So I brought Alice the tire repair kit from the spare tire drum, and Nettie brought the pliers and tire irons from the toolbox. The reporters stood around and watched.

Alice cranked our little jack to raise the wheel off the ground. She loosened the tire rings with the irons, pulled out the flat tube, and declared, "This is just like Mother takes the insides out of a turkey before stuffing it for Thanksgiving dinner."

She showed how to feel the inside of the tube for the hole that caused the flat. Then I roughed up the rubber so the cement would stick. Once the cement was tacky on both the tire and the patch, Alice held them together until the patch was set firm.

Of course, I already knew how to fix a flat. Alice was giving the lesson for the reporters, who were scribbling on their notepads.

Before she replaced the tube in its canvas tire, Alice felt carefully all around the inside of the tire to make sure there were no nails or tacks to cause another puncture. She dusted the tube with talcum powder, carefully stuffed it back in place, and replaced the tire rings.

Then Alice turned to the press boys and told them

the tire was ready for the pump. And they all took a turn.

The roads through the western part of Illinois are crunchy gravel, so we are making good time. The fields roll much more than in the eastern part of the state. Instead of newspaper folk, who have all departed, we are bothered by pigs. Yes, hogs, sows, and piglets roam all over the farm roadways. They pay so little mind to our new horn that we wonder if they are deaf.

De Kalb, Illinois, made famous as the home of the inventor of barbed wire, was a surprise: here, the post office roof is topped with a handsome copper dome, and the streets are lined with tall elm trees. It is very easy to pretend we are back in New Jersey again. Does this mean I am homesick?

Hotel food isn't too good around here.

Lots of burned hash, several days old. None of us is a fussy eater, though, so we fill up on sugar sandwiches—bread spread with butter and sugar. And we keep dreaming about our next home-cooked dinner.

June 24, 1909
Onward to Iowa   Mechanicsville, Iowa

Just through Dixon to Fulton, Illinois, we spotted the great, long bridge over the Mississippi. The wood planking over the Big River is barely wide enough for two wagons to pass. It is frightening to look down. Nettie and Maggie kept their eyes straight ahead. But Alice and I had to watch for gaps between the planks and for nailheads.

Here, on the other side, we are Out West! Though I must say being here isn't all that inspiring. This Iowa is a bathtub of mud. Late spring rains have left the roads like thick stew. I read somewhere that in the age of dinosaurs, this section between the Mississippi and the Missouri Rivers was underwater. It still is! The mud left behind may be wonderful for corn crops, but it is awful for motoring.

The first new blast of rain hit us in Mechanicsville, Iowa. We headed for the only shelter in sight, a livery stable. With flies buzzing around us and horses snorting and stomping, we waited for two hours for a letup in the storm. Then we ran with our muddy bags to the Page Hotel.

Alice started playing the Chickering piano in the dining room after supper, with rain still beating on the windows outside. If she doesn't stop showing off downstairs for the other guests, I will never get to sleep. Oh, no, here goes "Rock of Ages" again.

June 26, 1909
What Alice Forgot   at Weasel Creek, Iowa

Today we drove only 28 miles instead of the 130 to
150 we could drive back in New York. The roads are
bottomless puddles. Sometimes we can look at the
slope of the edges of a puddle and take a chance that
the water is low. But wherever Alice steers, there is no
way to avoid having at least one wheel slide down into
a hole. Alice says before this trip is over we'll all be
experts at taking apart roadside fences and borrowing
the rails for our wheels to ride out of the mud. Of
course we must always hammer the rails back when we
are done.

We plowed along in low gear today until the water in
our radiator boiled dry. Alice had forgotten to pack a
pail, so where were we going to get more water? We all
looked pretty dismal sitting there moaning, "Water,
water everywhere, but not a drop for our poor engine."

Then Nettie had an idea. She pulled her luggage
from under the tarp and dug around inside. "Aha," she
said, holding up her cut-glass cologne bottles with the
silver lids. Without a word, she and Maggie poured out
their expensive rosewater scents and began to dip the
fancy bottles into the nearest puddle. The biggest bot-
tle held perhaps half a cup.

"This water's not clean, but it's cool," Nettie said,
pouring it into the radiator. After 10 or 12 dips, our
engine hummed again.

Up ahead a beautiful team of horses and a large

farm wagon waited beside the road. A farm woman in a starched sunbonnet and a calico dress held the reins. As we drove near, she stood up tall in her wagon, straightened her bonnet, and asked us, "Are you those brave ladies who are driving from New York to San Francisco?"

When we said yes, she told us she was glad to meet us, since she'd read about us in the paper and had come six miles to see us for herself. I've heard of people dropping everything to watch the president ride by in a train, but to think anybody would go to that much trouble to look at us!

Nettie told her thank you for coming, just as if we were in the tea parlor. Then she poked me and said to wave and smile because it is best to be polite to strangers. So we all four waved and sat up proudly as we passed.

Once around the bend, Nettie and Maggie jumped down to fill our radiator again. After three more stops for puddle water, here we are at Weasel Creek.

June 27, 1909
Delayed by Flooding   Belle Plaine, Iowa

It seems like the patches of dry land are getting even farther apart. Yesterday the land around Weasel Creek was flooded. Alice thought the water might be shallow enough to drive through. She tugged on her rubber boots, took off her suit skirt, and pulled her petticoat forward between her legs and tucked it in the waistband of her bloomers. "This is Turkish style," she said, grabbing my umbrella to keep her balance and wading right in. Before we could blink, down she slipped into the brown water. It came up to her waist.

Alice was not the least bit startled. She simply remarked how lucky it was we hadn't tried to drive across before she made her test. All we could do now, she said, was eat a little supper and see if the water would go down after a bit. Then she told us she'd walk back to the last farm we passed and ask to buy bread and water.

Nettie was shocked to think Alice, muddy as she was, would go calling at a strange farmhouse. So I offered to go instead. Alice insisted I take the umbrella with me, because I might have to float in it! Maggie warned me to be careful of the pigs. They look cute, but a litter on the run can bump a person right into a ditch.

The piggies were well behaved. I brought back a lovely picnic for four—a loaf of white bread, a half pound of butter, a square comb of clover honey, and a jar of fresh water—all for 25 cents. We ate in the Maxwell and waited for Alice's petticoat to dry out a bit on the hood of the car, and for the water to go down.

Alice propped her feet on the dashboard and said it looked as if we'd have to spend the night in the car. She spread her lap robe and folded her arms beneath her head to make a pillow, admitting that it wasn't going to be easy to sleep with a steering wheel poking in her ribs. I put my feet up on the dashboard and looked for pictures of Greek myths in the stars.

We were awakened about four this morning by barking dogs, six or seven of them. They splattered mud in all directions as they dashed around our Maxwell. I was afraid they'd jump inside with us. Who could tell how wild they were? Nettie started swinging my umbrella to scare them off, "Shoo, shoo," but the dogs acted as if they didn't even see us. Still barking, they headed on down the road.

The puzzle we never solved was, Whatever were they chasing? Alice quickly pointed out that the dogs were *chasing*, not *swimming*. That meant the water was down. We could see a clear stretch of road at last.

Also, Alice's petticoat was dry. Well, almost.

We got to Belle Plaine, Iowa, by eight o'clock for a real breakfast of oatmeal, eggs, and bacon at the cottage of a Mr. and Mrs. Herring. Then our hosts gave each of us a bag of sweet, ripe cherries for the road to Boone.

There's no more time to write— we're off again.

Add a little water and this Nebraska road will turn into mud stew.

There were other guests at breakfast today in Boone, Iowa. Most were men, and they were full of warnings and advice like, "If I were you women, I'd put that Maxwell on a flatcar and ship it down to Omaha, Nebraska," "The mud isn't going to get any better," and "You ought to take the train." Those crosspatch farmers sounded just like Cousin Kermit.

Alice told them no thank you. She had promised to drive every inch of the way. It would be cheating to put the Maxwell on the railway for part of the journey.

The farmers laughed and told her to wait until she hit Danger Hill. They said Danger Hill has a 90-degree turn at the bottom. That means you can't get up steam and make a run for it uphill. They also said our load was too heavy to get all the way up to the top. Other cars have slid back down, turned around, and then tried to climb up Danger Hill in reverse.

Nettie spoke up and volunteered for the three of us—Maggie, me, and herself—to take our bags off and go to Omaha by train. Then Alice would drive up the hill. And everyone would hear about it.

Before I could argue, Nettie said there would be room for J. D. Murphy, the newsman from the *Boston Herald*, to ride along with Alice, since he weighed a lot less than Nettie and Maggie and I and all our luggage. "That way," she said, "he can write up a story when Alice reaches the top. Then the 'doubting Thomases' can really have something to talk about."

So here I am, stuck on this smoky train to Omaha. I don't know whether I'll ever tell Cousin Kermit about this part of the trip. I am boiling mad, and I don't like this plan at all. I don't see why I couldn't stay with Alice. I almost wish we'd get stopped by a gang like in that moving picture show *The Great Train Robbery*. The best part was when the actor fired his gun right into the audience. Everybody screamed, and some even fainted. That was pretty exciting for only a nickel.

All Nettie can talk about is having herself a tenderloin steak in Omaha and whether it will taste as good as food at Delmonico's back in New York City. Maggie plans to buy herself some Jergen's hand lotion. La-di-da!

June 29, 1909
Still Waiting in Omaha   Omaha, Nebraska

I must have read each letter from home a dozen times . . . two from Momma and Poppa, one from Homer (my much-older brother), and two from Aunt Claire. Everyone asks "How-Are-You" over and over. From what I can tell, nothing much is happening back there. So I'm glad I'm here, but what's taking Alice so long to meet us?

It gets tiresome down in the hotel lobby hour after hour. The confectionery store is next door, so Maggie sends me over to bring back sweets. We've tested every kind: lemon drops, peppermint drops, sourballs, peanut brittle, and black jelly beans. My favorite is this new Fleer's Blibber Blubber. You don't swallow it; you chew it, and then you can blow bubbles like blowing up balloons. Really! Nettie doesn't approve. The bubbles are awfully sticky when they pop on your clothes. Maggie showed me how to wear my collar tucked in to hide the splotch.

More News—Alice and J. D. arrived this very afternoon. While Alice left to wash her hair, J. D. told us about climbing Danger Hill. He said after they turned the corner and started up, smooth as you please, they saw another motorcar in trouble about two-thirds of the way up. That car's motor was coughing and spitting. The driver got out several times with a shovel to knock mud off the wheels. His car stalled again and again, but luckily his brakes held.

Alice shouted up the hill to the other driver that she had a rope and could pull him up. J. D. said, "Gosh-all-hemlock-Alice-what-do-you-think-you're-doing?" The driver said yes, please help, so Alice pressed her pedal hard and drove up until she was just past the stalled car.

Alice told the other driver to put his motor in low gear so her engine wouldn't be pulling dead weight. She tied her rear axle to the front hook of the other motorcar. It was slippery going, but tire chains kept both cars on Danger Hill road all the way to the top.

I'm sorry I missed watching that tow.

Alice and J. D. celebrated their climb with angel food cake at a boardinghouse outside Grand Junction. And a seamstress at Harlan sold Alice a new linen duster overcoat. Now she looks fresher than any of us for the next leg of our journey.

It has taken 13 days of driving to cross one muddy state.

July 10, 1909
Nuisances in Nebraska   Grand Island, Nebraska

We spent July 4 waiting out the rain in Sioux City, Iowa. There were red, white, and blue banners across the hotel desk, but I missed lighting those black fireworks snakes and drawing pictures in the air with sparkler sticks. Everything thereabouts was drenched.

Nebraska's roads aren't any better than Iowa's. We've been towed out of holes twice in one mile. We've been soaked with more rain and battered with hailstorms since we left Iowa. Then, about four miles from Grand Island, Nebraska, the right half of the rear axle broke. I almost toppled into the backseat. We had to catch a ride back to town on a passing lumber wagon, squeakity squeak. There's sawdust in my shoes. Thanks to the miracle of the telephone, a new axle was ordered. It arrives day after tomorrow by train. Hurray for modern times!

July 11, 1909
Ranchland Fences   Overton, Nebraska

Alice and a local mechanic had our new axle installed by 9 P.M. last night. Today we've been bumping along cattle and horse trails, following the telegraph wires west, since there are no real roads and we have no map. "After all," Alice says, "these poles and wires MUST lead us to the next town."

The grass out here ripples like an ocean blowing around us. We have been crossing miles and miles of sheep and cattle ranches. This was the old Overland stage route of years ago.

I have a new job: opening and closing the fence gates as we drive through the fields.

July 12, 1909
Law in the West   *Ogallala, Nebraska*

Men and horses blocked our way to Ogallala, Nebraska, today. At first we were afraid it was a holdup. My heart pounded in my ears.

One of the riders was dressed in black all over. Not a good sign, since I know the good guy in a moving picture usually dresses in white. He asked us where we'd come from. Alice cut off the engine and told him we'd driven from New York and were bound for San Francisco. He frowned at our Maxwell as if he couldn't believe we'd gotten this far.

Next he asked us if we had any guns (the same question the reporters asked us in New York). This time, I was afraid these men might be stealing firearms from travelers.

After he was satisfied we didn't have a gun, the man in black showed us a silver star badge pinned to his inside vest. A real western sheriff! Then he told us to wait. He turned his horse and headed back to the other riders. Alice shouted after him that he hadn't explained *why* we had to wait. Nettie yanked a lock of Alice's hair to get her to hush. Maggie whispered to Alice to hold her tongue.

Over his shoulder, the lawman shouted back the reason was a little murder. MURDER? Oh deary me! Deary us!

Those horsemen kept us waiting there in the heat for two hours. None of them spoke to us once in all that time. So this is the way a sheriff's posse solves a crime. How could they think WE might have murdered anyone?

One of the men from the posse finally came galloping back. "All right. You can go," he said. Alice wanted to know why the sheriff made us wait so long. The reason he gave us was that a man from "down the wash," wherever that is, was robbed and murdered in his cabin. The posse rider would not say one word more.

We cranked up the engine and got away from there, hoping the murderer went the other way. Wherever he went, he had more than a two-hour head start.

July 13, 1909
On the Streets of Cheyenne   Cheyenne, Wyoming

We can't help staring at the Indians, cowboys, and cattlemen here in Cheyenne, Wyoming, and they stare right back at us. By wiring ahead, J. D. had made sure a pilot car was waiting at the Inter-Ocean Hotel to lead us to California, since there are no direction signboards on the way and telegraph wires are far between. Our guides will show us the correct trail through the uncharted Rocky Mountains. Cousin Kermit once warned me to watch out for mountain lions if we ever got to the Rockies. But he'll say anything to annoy.

One of the reporters at the hotel told us the murder back in Ogallala had been solved. Quick work! A merchant became suspicious when a man and his wife started spending money like chicken feed in a nearby town. When the sheriff walked the murdered man's dog past the couple, the animal pounced on them, barking and biting. The reporter claimed that any jury out West would view the dog's attack as a sure sign of guilt. I wonder, how can they know for certain? Maybe the man had bacon grease on his fingers and the dog wanted a taste. Maggie says I dream up too many questions.

No sooner did we begin to climb the lower foothills outside Cheyenne than we had to pull the guide car out of an irrigation ditch with our block and tackle. Alice put the Maxwell in reverse and hoisted them out. Who's here to rescue who? I mean whom.

July 15, 1909	*near the*
Careful Timing	*North Platte River,*
between Trains	*Wyoming*

At Ramsey, Wyoming (no relation to Alice), the road bridge across the North Platte River had been washed away in a flood. The only way across was a railroad track on a trestle bridge 20 feet above the water. The innkeeper back in town told us we'd need an official

What a turnabout! Our trusty Maxwell comes to the rescue of the guide car.

permit from the stationmaster to cross the bridge, because Alice had to drive between train crossing times. Otherwise, we'd end up wrecked at the bottom of the Platte. And so would the train.

But guess where the station house was? Three-quarters of a mile away, on the OTHER side of the trestle. You had to cross it first to get a permit to cross it. This surely is a backwards world!

I had the idea that Alice should stay in the Maxwell while the three of us walked over the trestle to get the permit. Nettie and Maggie could talk to the stationmaster. I would wait just on the other side of the bridge and wave to Alice when Nettie signaled that he had signed the permit.

Maggie wanted to know what to do if a train came while we were crossing on foot. I told her that we'd dive in for a swim and she should keep her ears open for the whistle.

Maggie and Nettie picked up their skirts and hopped over those railroad ties like jackrabbits. They were already pounding on the station door before I got even halfway across the trestle. Then it took a full hour for the stationmaster to telegraph up and down the line to make sure trains were moving on schedule.

At last he signed the permit. As we had agreed, Maggie next waved to me. I signaled to Alice, and she began to bump across the tracks, the left wheels between the two rails, the right wheels between the rail and the narrow edge of the trestle. First Alice fed a little gas, then she let out the clutch, then came a bump, then she hit the brake. One bump at a time, up and down, for three-quarters of a mile, all the way across the bridge.

By the time Alice got to our side, I could see she was frowning from some awful pain. "Oh, Minna, I have appendicitis," she moaned and sat on the roadside, her head down in her lap.

Nettie and Maggie came running, squawking about finding a doctor, about how people could die from appendicitis, about how we would have to cancel the journey, and on and on. But in a few minutes, Alice lifted her head, began to smile, and said she felt quite a bit better: "I think I must have had a sudden bad case of jolt-itis." When she laughed again like the old Alice, we were all relieved.

July 16, 1909
Cliffs and Ravines

Bitter Creek, Wyoming

We've been climbing slowly, slowly toward the Continental Divide—that's the highest point in the Rocky Mountains. Our guides have turned back, nursing a weak axle. They warned us to stop often and cool the motor. Coyotes are yowling nearby. All around us are buttes—those are squatty flat-topped hills—and rocky cliffs. The alkali lakes are not fit to drink because they are full of mineral salts. You can hardly bear to smell them, much less taste. The arroyos—cracks wide

Here I am, standing on the running board, scanning the trail ahead. I don't know if I look like an American pioneer, but I feel like one!

47

enough to swallow us up—are as deep as 60 feet, sometimes with water at the bottom. It would be foolish to travel after dark. Boom we'd go, down to Doom.

As Alice steers the Maxwell up steep inclines, Nettie, Maggie, and I stand beside the car with blocks of wood. Alice presses the gas pedal in low gear and pulls ahead for a few inches. We shove the blocks behind the rear wheels so they won't slide back. Then Alice inches up some more. This way, we climb to the crest of each rising hill. "You're getting a week's worth of exercise all at once," Alice tells us. I'd say it's more like a couple months' worth.

July 17, 1909
Bad Night's Sleep   Opal, Wyoming

We were worn out when we checked in last night at the only hotel in Opal, Wyoming. The room clerk led us up to the second floor and showed Nettie and Maggie to their room, Alice and me to ours. I must have fallen into the sheets before I took my shoes off. Sometime in the night I began to twitch and whine in my sleep—at any rate, that's what woke Alice.

I opened my eyes with Alice shaking me, asking what was the matter. I told her I didn't know, but I surely was itchy all over.

Alice threw back my covers, lit the kerosene lamp, touched the raised red spots as big as quarters breaking out on my legs and arms, and exclaimed, "Bedbugs!"

She rolled me out of my bed and said we were going to get out of that room for certain and as soon as possible.

Maggie and Nettie seemed to be sleeping soundly in the room next door, so we didn't wake them. We tip-toed down the stairs into the hotel office, but there wasn't a soul in sight. There was no bell to ring. One

Out West, the telegraph wires show us the way to go.

lamp was still lit near a blackboard listing numbers of empty rooms—in case a guest should arrive after the clerk went to bed. There were no keys. All of them must have been lost long ago. We thought about trying one of the empty rooms, but were afraid to risk more bugs.

Alice was bothered just thinking some sheepherder might wander into the wrong unlocked room. We agreed we were better off down in the office. The only furniture was a round table and a few plain wooden chairs. So we slept sitting up, our heads resting on the table.

This morning when the owners reappeared, no one asked why we were there. Does this happen all the time, I wonder? Maggie and Nettie got no bites at all, but Nettie laid us out in lavender for not waking and warning them. At least they're not suffering today from cricks in the neck.

July 23, 1909
Making Ready
for the Desert   Salt Lake City, Utah

At Salt Lake City, Utah, we picked up more mail from home, including another letter from Cousin Kermit. He wrote me two sentences—"Dear Minna, I doubt that you have gotten this far. But if you have, you will probably soon die of thirst in the desert." I'll bet HE's dying of jealousy.

We took a few days off for car repairs and for swimming in rented bathing costumes in the Great Salt Lake. We floated like toy boats in a tub. It took many dunkings in fresh water to wash the salt off. By tomorrow, all the springs under the car will be oiled and wrapped in burlap for protection as we cross the desert.

July 24, 1909
Prairie Dogs   *Orr's Ranch, Utah*

The trail through Utah is full of prairie dog holes. They stretch ahead of us for miles. As we ride over the low hills, thousands of heads pop out of the ground ahead to see us, then pop back down. They must feel the earth shake before we pass by. Alice lay face down on the sand to try to get a picture of one, but the little creatures never failed to pop up in an altogether different hole, then grin and disappear again.

51

Often there are just two dusty tracks for our wheels. Alice steered carefully all morning. Then at noon we hit our first prairie dog hole. A bolt flew out of the tie-rod connecting the wheels, and the front of the car collapsed. We all tipped forward. Alice got out, slid under the Maxwell's back wheels, and tied everything back together with baling wire and Maggie's extra hairpins until we could reach the blacksmith forge at Orr's Ranch.

July 29, 1909
Another Delay   Callao, Utah

Out West we've learned to watch for dark clouds, because a cloudburst can mean a sudden flood ripping along the ravines and trailways, pulling us underwater. As we were leaving Callao, we had to change plans quickly when our road disappeared into a gaping hole still filled with swirling water from a recent rainstorm. Then, while trying to cross another gullywasher safely, we lost another axle. Because it will take three whole days for a new one to be shipped from San Francisco, Alice will wait in Callao to oversee repairs, and Nettie, Maggie, and I are catching the noon stage to Ely, Nevada. Nettie says Ely is known for its copper mines.

From prairie dog holes (above) to gullywashers (left), we can't seem to keep the Maxwell in one piece.

July 30, 1909
Ironing Secrets
Ely, Nevada

Alice and the Maxwell have arrived! We've lost precious time waiting for the new axle. Finally a local blacksmith made a copy that works. Alice spent endless hot hours around a forge, covering her ears while the smith hammered pieces to fit. And many more pieces that didn't fit.

Meanwhile, here at Ely, we've written letters home and watched our first Chinese laundryman at work. First he sipped about a fourth of a glass of water, then he sprinkled the clean clothes by spitting out a spray over all the wrinkled wash. Now that I know about the way people iron in the West, I don't think I will ever again have my clothes cleaned out here. I had a good mind to wash them over, but there wasn't time.

P.S. Maggie has just told me Nettie rinsed out the nightdress the laundryman ironed for her!

July 31, 1909
Crossing the Desert
Eureka, Nevada

We are more than 200 miles from California, and we still have more desert to cross. Cousin Kermit should see the South African bag Alice bought at Ely for our drinking water. It is a one-gallon size envelope of heavy canvas, 10 x 16 inches, with a cork attached by a cord so the stopper can't be lost. When the bag is filled with water and hung from the auto, the slow seeping and evaporation of water through the canvas cools the water that's still inside. This bag will also provide us with refills for our radiator.

We have let some air out of our tires because the sand will be hot, and hot air swells the tubes. We will also raise the sides of the front hood and turn them under. It will be noisy riding behind an open engine, but perhaps the motorworks will not overheat so quickly if they stay uncovered. To keep as cool as possible, we will travel early—up at 5 A.M.—and late in the evening, since the moon is waxing full.

Rolling over the sand, we try to dodge the prickly little horned toads and clumps of tumbleweed sagebrush blowing across our path. Hot air waves rise in front of us. The cactuses seem to be dancing before our eyes.

I thought I was dreaming when a dozen Indians on horseback appeared, all with drawn bows and arrows. They were dressed in head feathers and trousers but were bare from the waist up. Alice and I grabbed hands and held on tight. I closed my eyes, waiting for the first arrows to zing past. My brain told me that this was 1909, and most stories about Indians were pure poppycock. But my heart went down to my feet. Would this be the terrible end of our cross-country adventure? To get so close to our goal—and now this dreadful ambush?

After a few minutes and still no war whoops, I squinted into the sunset to see the whole group suddenly wheel around as a jackrabbit leaped 20 feet across the roadway. The Indians followed the rabbit southwest to our left, never slowing down or paying us any attention. The four of us felt foolish as dunces. We had frightened ourselves for no reason at all. We drove to the right, northwest to Eureka, Nevada, arriving at 11 P.M.

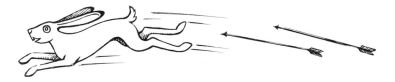

August 2, 1909
Favorite Breakfast   Reno, Nevada

Before we started out at 5:30 this morning, we were served a never-to-be-forgotten breakfast of lamb chops and chocolate cake.

I do not recommend August in the desert. Too hot and sleepy to write. We passed through Rawhide, Fallon, Hazen, Fernley, Wadsworth, and—after dark—Sparks, a little town with so much electric power that it seems to light up the whole desert! Sparks even has trolley service to Reno, about two miles away. It is midnight in Reno, at the Riverside Hotel. I am turning in now for another long drink of water and a short night.

In Reno we stayed at the Riverside Hotel (top), but there was no time to take the trolley (bottom) to Sparks. California was waiting for us!

August 3, 1909   on the shores of Lake Tahoe,
The Sierra Range   California

It's been uphill to Carson City, Nevada, where we ate
lunch in a Japanese restaurant looking out on the golden
dome of the capitol building. The waiter said there had
been another earthquake last week in San Francisco,
but not a serious one like three years ago. To tell the
truth, I think it would be exciting to feel the ground
shake, so long as the buildings stayed up.

We have started to climb the steep, sandy road up
the Sierra Nevada. At each double-back turn, we stop
to rest the Maxwell and admire the view of blue skies
and distant purple peaks. Our sturdy motor pulls us up
past summit after summit. As we neared the east shore
of Lake Tahoe, the trees grew suddenly plentiful and
green. There are sugar pines, Douglas firs, and the very
famous redwoods, which make me feel smaller than a
thimble under a flagpole. "What a land!" Alice
exclaimed. "What mountains, what blue skies, what
clear, sparkling water!"

The Maxwell people have paid for an overnight at a
lovely cottage for four on the south tip of Lakeside Park.
Is there anywhere more beautiful than this? I am writing tonight to the soft sound of pine needles brushing
the roof. It took us eight hours to cover 70 miles today,
and we're still going up. Eleven more miles 'til we reach
the pass at Meyers, California.

August 5, 1909
Here We Are   *Hayward, California*

We wound down through Placerville, which is also
known as Hangtown. There used to be so much crime
and lawlessness in gold mining days, 30 or 40 years ago,
that men were hanged here in pairs. So said the Mannix
family in Sacramento, where we spent last night.

Today we made Stockton, where we were joined by a
parade of the other six autos in town. Everyone cheered
our trusty Maxwell. At Hayward we enjoyed a snack of
cheese omelettes and hot tamales, which are like corn-
meal rolls cooked around meat and wrapped in corn
shucks. Fun to eat, but don't bite into the shucks. We
could easily make it to San Francisco later tonight, but
the Maxwell salesmen don't want us to arrive after dark.
Picture taking works better in daylight. Funny how you
have to think about things like this if you want to get
better attention in the newspaper.

My go-to-town hat has been smashed in the suitcase.
Nettie and Maggie bought some silk chiffon net in
Hayward, and they are stitching it across the crown so
I will look festive in the photographs tomorrow. They
really can be nice—and I've almost forgotten the times
Nettie seemed so cross.

August 6, 1909
Arrival Day!! San Francisco, California

We awoke this morning all jittery and happy, but sad at the same time. We were 100-percent glad we made it but regretted the trip would soon be over. Maggie says this feeling is called "bittersweet," like the chocolate.

There were only 20 more miles to go until we reached the ferry house at Oakland, where we would board a boat taking us across the wide, blue bay to San Francisco. Time sped by too quickly. We arrived at the Oakland boat dock within an hour after breakfast. Once on the ferry, we set the Maxwell's brakes and raced to the front end of the boat to watch San Francisco bobbing in the water. Great golliwogs! To think that those same Pacific Ocean waves touch the shores of the Chinese Empire!

Our ferry slid out into the bay. Gulls were squawking like New York street vendors. Buoys were clanging. We heard foghorns hoot, though there was no fog. The other passengers seemed very excited to get a look at the Maxwell and us. Who told them I don't know, but everyone knew where we were from and what Alice had done. We did not have a single quiet moment, as every rider wanted to congratulate us.

On the San Francisco wharf, our ferry bumped against the pilings and rocked a little. The captain unhooked the chains across the bow of the ferry. I jumped down and gave the good old Maxwell's crank the last twirl of this trip, hopping aboard as we rolled

We made it! What a glorious feeling. Here we all are in San Francisco: (left to right) me, Alice, Nettie, and Maggie.

down the ramp to the dock. "Straighten your cap, Alice," the three of us shouted.

Almost two months since leaving New York City, we at last puttered slowly onto San Francisco's Market Street. All around us were cheers and honks of welcome and so many people you could hardly tell there'd been a big earthquake here only three years ago. What a hubbub! Now I know firsthand what the word "hubbub" means. There was a lineup of other Maxwells, photographers, pressmen, and presswomen too, all wanting to meet Alice and shake her hand. We had come 3,800 miles on 11 tire changes and three axles in only 59 days, faster—for all our delays—than either of the two men driving across country before us. Aren't we proud? Everyone hereabouts is calling Alice "Woman Motorist of the Century."

A reporter took me aside and asked if I would ever take this trip again. Who wouldn't say yes? I want my cousin Kermit to see what great adventure is like. And next time, I'LL drive.

As Alice told the reporters today, it looks like automobiles are here to stay!

Cousin Kermit took a big bite—not a little nibble—
out of his straw boater today, but after a while, I let him
spit it out.

AFTERWORD

Alice and the Maxwell returned to New Jersey by express train. Hermine, Nettie, and Maggie stayed in San Francisco a few days longer to "take in the sights."

During World War I Alice organized the Red Cross Motor Corps for Camp Merritt in Dumont, New Jersey. After the war she drove her children on visits to the national parks, making at least 30 more trips across the country.

By 1961, the year Alice wrote her memoir of the auto trip, both Minna and Maggie had died, but 101-year-old Nettie Powell Lewis was still alive. At her death in 1983 at age 96, Alice had been driving more than 80 years. She received only one traffic ticket—for making an illegal U-turn. Alice's husband, John, a congressman from New Jersey, never drove, but was regularly her passenger. The question he asked her most often was, "How do you stop this thing?"

Alice remembers her cross-country adventure.

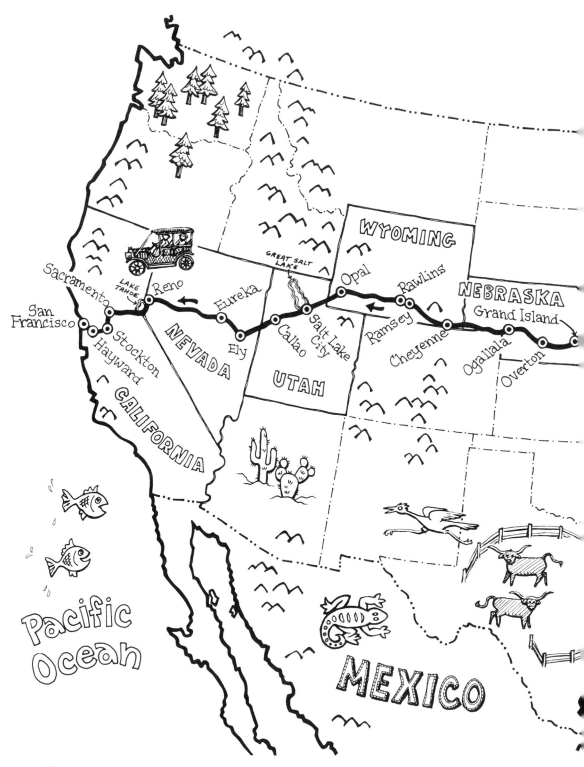

WYOMING

GREAT SALT
LAKE

Opal

Rawlins

NEBRASKA

Sacramento

LAKE
TAHOE

Reno

Eureka

Ramsey

Cheyenne

Grand Island

San
Francisco

NEVADA

Ely

Callao

Salt Lake
City

Ogallala

Stockton

Hayward

Overton

CALIFORNIA

UTAH

Pacific
Ocean

MEXICO

CANADA

LAKE SUPERIOR

LAKE HURON

LAKE MICHIGAN

NEW YORK

L. ONTARIO

Amsterdam

Poughkeepsie

Auburn

Buffalo

LAKE ERIE

New York City

Ashtabula

Cleveland

Chicago

Toledo

OHIO

Rochelle

INDIANA

Mechanicsville

ILLINOIS

MISSISSIPPI R.

Grand Junction

Sioux City

Boone

Belle Plain

Omaha

IOWA

MISSISSIPPI RIVER

MOO!

MOO!

Atlantic Ocean

67

A FEW CAR QUESTIONS

When were the first American cars made?
The first vehicles resembling what we think of as cars date from about the 1860s, and they were strictly experimental. Many never made it out the blacksmith's door.

A steam-powered automobile invented by two brothers, James A. and Henry Alonzo House, carried 13 lucky passengers from Bridgeport to a boat launching in Stratford, Connecticut, in 1866.

In 1891 William Morrison designed the first electric car, which required 10 hours to charge the battery, and could run for 13 hours at a speed of 14 miles per hour.

The first successful gasoline-powered car in the United States was built in 1893 and was driven on the streets of Springfield, Massachusetts, by two brothers, Charles E. and J. Frank Duryea.

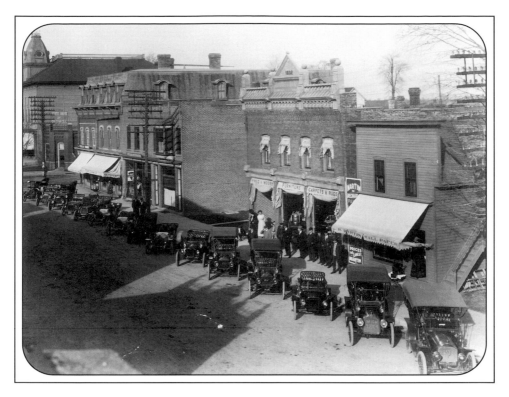

Automobiles lined up on the street in Croswell, Michigan, in 1909

How many cars were there in Alice Ramsey's home town?

In the spring of 1908, there were half a dozen automobiles in Hackensack, New Jersey.

How many cars were there in the United States in 1909 when Alice Ramsey made her famous trip?

There were 300,000 cars registered in the United States in 1909. This sounds like a lot—but half of them had been bought that very year, and we can presume many sold due to publicity about Alice's trip. Most of the cars counted in this census were only two to three years old or newer because these early fragile autos rattled themselves apart after only a few thousand miles. Road accidents in these unpredictable machines (new drivers crashing into trees, creeks, and fences) were not uncommon.

By 1911, three years after the Model T Ford was introduced and two years after Alice's historic trip, there were more than 600,000 automobiles registered. That's double the number the year Alice drove to San Francisco.

Where did drivers get fuel?

Typically, gasoline was sold at a pump at the curb of a general store or a blacksmith shop. There were no service stations as we know them—most people still traveled by horse. Repairs were made by farm tool dealers in the country or by bicycle shops or by carriage makers in town.

How many gas stations were there?

The first published census of gasoline pumps was made 10 years after Alice's drive, in 1918-19, after the end of World War I. At that time there were 15,000 pumps across the nation, with most concentrated on the eastern seaboard. Gasoline was supplied to these pumps in tank trucks, a result of wartime manufacturing know-how.

BIBLIOGRAPHY

Automobile Quarterly, 18 (1970): 136-139.

Freericks, Mary. "Alice Huyler Ramsey." *In Past and Promise: Lives of New Jersey Women*, edited by Joan N. Burstyn, 183-185. Metuchen, N.J.: Scarecrow Press, 1990.

Georgano, G. N. *The Complete Encyclopedia of Motorcars 1885 to the Present*. New York: E. P. Dutton Inc., 1968.

Kane, Joseph Nathan. *Famous First Facts*. New York: H. W. Wilson Co., 1981.

Kimes, Beverly Rae, and Henry Austin Clark Jr. *Standard Catalog of American Cars, 1805-1942*. Iola, Wis.: Krause Publications, 1985.

Kuralt, Charles. *On the Road with Charles Kuralt*. New York: G. P. Putnam's Sons, 1985.

Langworth, Richard M. *The Complete History of Chrysler Corporation*. New York: Beekman Publishers Inc., 1985.

Lent, Henry B. *Car of the Year—1895-1970*. New York: E. P. Dutton Inc., 1970.

Pettifer, Julian, and Nigel Turner. *Automania: Man and the Motorcar*. Boston: Little, Brown & Co., 1984.

Ramsey, Alice Huyler. *Veil, Duster, and Tire Iron*. Pasadena, Calif.: Castle Press, 1961.

Newspaper Articles

Bergen Record. September 13, 1983.

Los Angeles Times. February 19, 1961; June 16, 1966; March 5, 1971.

Oakland Tribune. August 6, 1909.

The illustrations are reproduced through the courtesy of: pp. 2, 6, 12, 26, 61, front cover, back cover, Detroit Public Library Automotive History Collection; pp. 10, 20, 23, 65, American Automobile Manufacturers Association; pp. 28, 45, 47, 49, 53 (top and bottom), the Free Library of Philadelphia, Automotive Reference Collection; p. 36, Nebraska State Historical Society; p. 57 (top and bottom), Nevada Historical Society; p. 69, Library of Congress.